Lizzie And Charley Go Shopping

DYAN SHELDON

WALKER BOOKS
AND SUBSIDIARIES
LONDON · BOSTON · SYDNEY

To Lizzie and Charlie

First published 1999 by Walker Books Ltd
87 Vauxhall Walk, London SE11 5HJ

This edition published 2000

2 4 6 8 10 9 7 5 3 1

Text © 1999 Dyan Sheldon
Cover illustration © 1999 Nick Sharratt

This book has been typeset in Plantin.

Printed in England by Clays Ltd, St Ives plc

British Library Cataloguing in Publication Data
A catalogue record for this book is
available from the British Library.

ISBN 0-7445-6978-8

Contents

Mrs Moscos Gives Lizzie a Warning

....

Lizzie checked to make sure that her birthday money was in the change compartment of her purple bag, then she swung the bag over her shoulder, opened the front door and stepped into the sunny afternoon.

"And where are you going on this beautiful day, Miss Lizzie Wesson?" asked the hedge that separated the Wessons' front garden from the front garden next door. "To see the pink city of Jaipur or Machu Picchu, the lost city of the Incas?"

"Hi, Mrs Moscos," said Lizzie. She leaned over the hedge. Mrs Moscos, the Wessons' next-door neighbour, was on her knees, tending her vegetables. All Lizzie could see of her was the top of her enormous red straw sun hat and the bottoms of her neon-pink trainers. Everyone else on Lizzie's road grew things like daffodils and roses in their front gardens, but Mrs Moscos grew tomatoes and potatoes. She was a refugee from somewhere in Eastern Europe and prided herself on being a very practical person.

"Well?" insisted Mrs Moscos. "What is it to be today? The Falls of Niagara or the seas of the moon?"

"Charley and I are going to the shopping centre," Lizzie informed Mrs Moscos's hat. Charley Desoto was Lizzie's best friend. She lived a few houses down, on the other side of Meteor Drive.

"Tut-tut-tut," said Mrs Moscos, digging at the soil. "You don't want to go shopping. You have a whole universe at your disposal, Lizzie Wesson. What you want to do is have an adventure."

"No, I don't," answered Lizzie. "I've saved all the money I got for my birthday. What I want is a really special top to go with the black skirt my parents gave me."

Mrs Moscos continued to dig.

"Why spend such a beautiful day in a shopping centre?" she asked. "Can you not hear the galaxies calling you?"

"No," said Lizzie. "All I hear's the traffic and Mr Whisper's telly."

Mr Whisper lived in the house on the other side of Mrs Moscos's. He was a refugee from somewhere in Eastern Europe, too, but unlike Mrs Moscos he was quiet and minded his own business. His real name wasn't Whisper, but no one on Meteor Drive could pronounce his real name. He was known as Mr Whisper because he talked so softly and kept to himself. The only way anyone knew he was there was the TV that played continually whenever he was home.

Mrs Moscos looked up from under her hat. Even when Mrs Moscos was looking straight at her, Lizzie always had the feeling that she was seeing something else.

"Shopping centres are very unhealthy," said Mrs Moscos firmly. "All those people breathing that recycled air and…"

"Charley and I like shopping," said Lizzie quickly, hoping to stop Mrs Moscos before she got into the full swing of what was wrong with shopping centres. Mrs Moscos wore her red straw hat whenever she went outdoors, even in winter, because she was very sensitive to the sun. She didn't go to the shopping centre because she was very sensitive to the air, the germs, the light and the music. She ate only fresh, organic vegetables because she was very sensitive to additives and pesticides. "Shopping's fun," Lizzie added. She smiled brightly at the straw hat.

"Fun..." Mrs Moscos shook her head slowly. "Fun is going out and doing things, not going out and buying things."

Not only did Mrs Moscos grow onions instead of pansies, she seemed to disapprove of most of the things that her neighbours approved of, shopping when you didn't actually need anything being one of them.

"Well," Lizzie said, still smiling brightly. "I have to get Charley. I'll see you later."

Mrs Moscos looked up at her. "Tell me one thing before you speed away, please, Lizzie Wesson," she ordered. "Tell me if you and Charley will be going to Happy Burger while you're at the shopping centre."

"What?" Lizzie blinked in bewilderment. She hadn't realized that Happy Burger was another of the things Mrs Moscos didn't approve of.

Mrs Moscos glanced over her shoulder as Mr Whisper's front door opened and Mr Whisper himself emerged. He was a tall, thin man, pale and stooped, who looked very much how a whisper would look in human form. He was wearing the grey suit, broad-brimmed grey hat and grey gloves he always wore and the black umbrella he always carried was tucked under one arm.

Mrs Moscos bowed her head towards the garden again. "Will you be going to Happy Burger?" she asked more softly, yanking another weed from the earth and tossing it into her green wicker basket. "Because if I were you, Lizzie Wesson, I'd think two times about going to Happy Burger today, maybe even three…"

Lizzie sighed. "I will," she promised, edging her way towards the gate. "But I really have to hurry. Charley and I are meeting my sister at the bus stop. She'll leave without us if we're late."

Mrs Moscos glanced over her shoulder again as Mr Whisper started down his front path. "I mean it, Lizzie Wesson," she hissed almost urgently. "You and Charley should stay out of Happy Burger. It's a dangerous place to be today."

Lizzie nodded, only half listening. "Sure, Mrs Moscos. But I really really have to go … my sister…"

"Are you paying attention to me?" demanded Mrs Moscos. "This is important, Lizzie. You must stay out of Happy Burger, no matter what."

"I will," promised Lizzie. "Really, I will." She would have agreed to anything, even cleaning her room, if it meant getting away.

"Of course you will," said Mrs Moscos. She watched over her shoulder as Mr Whisper stepped through his front gate. "Go, go…" she said suddenly, waving a yellow glove in Lizzie's direction. "Don't let me keep you and Charley from your destiny."

Lizzie had no idea what Mrs Moscos meant by "Don't let me keep you and Charley from your destiny", but, as usual when she didn't understand something, she didn't ask for an explanation. She pretended she knew what Mrs Moscos was talking about and hurried on her way.

Mr Whisper had turned the corner and Lizzie was across the road when she heard Mrs Moscos call after her.

"Remember!" shouted Mrs Moscos, "Think two or three times!"

Lizzie and Charley
Don't Get to Shop

Allie Wesson's voice boomed through the small shop as though it were on the tannoy.

"Will you two come on! We don't have all day, you know!"

Everyone, including Lizzie and Charley, turned round.

Lizzie's sister was standing at the entrance with her best friend, Gemma. Both of them had their hands full of carrier bags and scowls on their faces.

"Oh, no…" groaned Lizzie. "The Gruesome Twosome strikes again. We haven't even had a chance to look at anything yet. I'll never get a new top at this rate."

Allie and Gemma had been marching Lizzie and Charley in and out of shops all afternoon. Because of the last time the four of them went shopping – the time Lizzie and

Charley got lost – Allie wouldn't let them out of her sight. Which meant that all they had done for the last three hours was watch Allie and Gemma try on clothes, and give their opinions when asked.

"Just a few more minutes," begged Lizzie. "Charley and I aren't ready to go."

Allie readjusted the red bag that contained her new dress. "Well, we are," she snapped. "We're tired of this place. Gemma and I want to go to that new boutique, Kosmickicks, on the other side of the mall. It's meant to be really cool."

"But I want to look for a top here!" wailed Lizzie.

Allie made a face. "Who's stopping you?"

"You are!" Lizzie made a worse face back.

Charley pinched Lizzie's arm. "Don't make her angry," she whispered. "Why don't you say we'll meet them later?"

Lizzie nodded. She gave her sister a pleasant smile. "Tell us where you'll be and we'll catch up."

Allie didn't return the smile.

"Oh, sure…" she screeched. "And then you and Charley get lost like last time, and Gemma and I spend the rest of the day trying to find you." Allie tossed her long dark curls over her shoulder. "I'm not getting in trouble again because of you two."

"You won't get into trouble," Lizzie promised. "Besides, now Charley and I know which bus to take." Unlike last time, when they'd ended up miles from home and had to phone Lizzie's father to come and get them. "We're not little kids, you know. We're ten."

Charley held up her left hand. "And we have watches," she chipped in.

Gemma, who never spoke to Lizzie or Charley unless it was to make a sarcastic remark, whispered into Allie's ear.

"Half an hour," said Allie, as though she were being incredibly generous. "We'll meet you in Kosmickicks, opposite the fountain."

Lizzie and Charley both nodded.

Lizzie held up her watch this time.

"Half an hour."

"In the new boutique opposite the fountain," put in Charley.

Allie pointed a finger at them. "I'm warning you, you little termites. If you're not there, we'll go home without you. And I'll tell Mum you deliberately walked off, then it'll be all your fault."

Lizzie and Charley were silent as they watched Allie and Gemma disappear into the crowd outside the store.

"Thank God they're gone," said Lizzie when Allie's dark head and Gemma's blonde one were no longer visible. "If I had to spend another five minutes with them I'd go mad."

"I'm glad I'm an only child." Charley made a sympathetic face. "I really feel sorry for you, Lizzie. I'd put myself up for adoption if Allie were my sister."

"I'd rather put *her* up for adoption," said Lizzie. "I like my parents. It's Allie I can't stand."

Lizzie Ignores Mrs Moscos's Warning

....

"It isn't fair," Lizzie grumbled as she and Charley pushed their way through the mob of afternoon shoppers that stood between them and Kosmickicks. "I still haven't found a top I like. I need more time."

"Well, we don't have more time," said Charley. "It's already after four-thirty. My mum'll kill me if we end up going home on our own again."

"I wouldn't mind if my mum killed me if I had a new top," Lizzie muttered. "At least I'd have something nice to be buried in."

"Oh, stop complaining," said Charley. "You've had ten more minutes than you should have had. Never mind my mother, your sister's going to kill us first."

The thought of being murdered by Allie temporarily put the new top out of Lizzie's head. Not only would her sister murder her, she would never take her and Charley shopping again. Lizzie picked up speed. "It'll be midnight before we get to the boutique at the rate *you're* going," she snapped.

"Don't start blaming me because we're late," gasped Charley from behind her. "I'm not the one who just *had* to try on one more thing."

Lizzie picked up more speed. "Well, I'm not the one who had to try on every necklace in the shop."

"That was only because I was so bored–" Charley broke off and grabbed Lizzie's shoulder. "Look! There's the fountain!"

Just visible above the heads of the crowd was a cloud of water. To the left of it a black sign proclaimed KOSMICKICKS – Intergalactic Clothes and Accessories – in large silver letters. Lizzie couldn't help feeling relieved. The only thing worse than not getting a new top would be not getting a new top and being left behind by Allie.

"And there's Kosmickicks!" Lizzie took

hold of Charley and pulled her towards the shining mini-skirts and iridescent tops that hung in the window on wires so thin the clothes seemed to be floating in the air.

"Wow…" breathed Lizzie, her eyes on the shimmering rainbow of outfits. "1 bet I could find what I want in there…"

"And I wish we could find what we want out here," said Charley.

Lizzie tore her eyes away from the window display. "What?"

"Your sister," said Charley with great patience. "She's not here."

"She'll be inside," Lizzie assured her. She turned towards the entrance, and froze. Just disappearing through the shining silver door of Kosmickicks was a tall, thin, grey figure with a black umbrella tucked under his arm.

"Did you see that?" Lizzie shook Charley's arm. "Charley, did you see what I just saw?"

But Charley's face was pressed against the window. "I don't see them inside either," she announced.

"Never mind them," insisted Lizzie. "I just saw Mr Whisper go into the boutique!"

Charley pulled away from the glass to look at Lizzie. "You're mad," she said flatly. "Mr Whisper would never go into a shop like this, and you know it. He doesn't even go to the supermarket."

Lizzie hated it when Charley was right. But it was true; Mr Whisper would never go into a shop like this. Lizzie's eyes wandered back to the clothes in the window. What would he possibly buy? The silver party dress? The sparkling blue halter? The black skirt spangled with stars? She grinned as she imagined Mr Whisper strolling down his front path in a mini-skirt and neon top, his grey hat on his head and his black umbrella under his arm.

Charley gave her a poke. "What are you laughing about? This is serious, Lizzie. What if Allie and Gemma have gone without us?"

"They're probably in the changing room," said Lizzie. She started towards the door again. She had to see what Mr Whisper was doing in Kosmickicks.

Mr Whisper, apparently, wasn't doing anything in Kosmickicks. There were girls looking through the racks of clothes, girls queued up at the cash register, girls rushing into and out of the changing rooms, but there was no middle-aged man with a black umbrella anywhere.

Charley's eyes were on the feet showing beneath the curtains of the changing cubicles. "They're not here," said Charley gloomily. "Not unless they've changed their shoes."

Lizzie wasn't listening, she was looking around for a rear exit. Maybe Mr Whisper had simply used the shop as a shortcut.

"Do you think we should ask one of the salesgirls?" asked Charley. "In case they remember seeing Allie and Gemma?"

Lizzie sighed. There was a fire exit at the back, but no one could have gone that way without setting off the alarm. It was as though the black and white floor of

Kosmickicks had opened up and swallowed Mr Whisper whole. Where could he have gone?

"You can ask if you want," said Lizzie, "but they won't remember." She gestured to a gaggle of teenagers shrieking over a row of silver trousers. "They all look exactly alike. And, anyway," she went on, "so what if they were here? They're not here now."

Lizzie and Charley waited by the fountain.

"I knew it," moaned Charley after ten minutes. "They've gone without us."

"Allie wouldn't dare go without us," said Lizzie confidently. "My parents cut her allowance for two weeks for leaving us last time. She's bluffing."

"Bluffing?" Charley looked hopeful. "You really think so?"

Lizzie laughed bitterly. "Positive."

If there was one person Lizzie knew well, it was Allie Wesson. It was just like Allie to pay Lizzie back for wandering off last time by arranging to meet at four-thirty and then not turning up until five. And while Lizzie and Charley were sitting there waiting, getting damp from the spray of the fountain, Allie and Gemma were shopping. Shopping and laughing at them for being such termites.

Thinking about all the things like this that Allie had done to her in the last ten years, Lizzie became furious. "I've had enough of being pushed around," she decided. "We're not going to let Allie get away with this."

Charley looked surprised. "We're not?"

Lizzie shook her head very firmly. "No, we're not. We're going to beat her at her own game for a change."

"And how are we going to do that?" Charley inquired with exaggerated politeness.

Lizzie pointed left. "We're going to Happy Burger, that's what we're going to do. Let them think we left without them. It'll do Allie good to get some of her own medicine."

A thoughtful expression came over Charley's face. "But I thought you said that Mrs Moscos told you not to go into Happy

Burger today," she reminded Lizzie.

Lizzie's eyes went from Charley to Happy Burger. Mrs Moscos's warning had been bizarre enough for her to tell Charley about it, but it didn't seem very important now. Happy Burger looked incredibly inviting, and besides, Lizzie was suddenly very thirsty. Allie hadn't let them stop for so much as a gulp of water.

"Oh, that…" Lizzie rolled her eyes. "You know how weird Mrs Moscos is. She probably read something in the paper about the drinks being too hot or somebody finding a hair in their Big Bun."

"She *is* weird, isn't she?" agreed Charley. "My mother says Mrs Moscos's from a different planet."

"Well, she is from Eastern Europe," said Lizzie. "I suppose that's pretty much the same thing."

Why Lizzie Should Have Listened to Mrs Moscos

....

Lizzie and Charley weren't the only ones who preferred shopping to having an adventure. As you would expect from the world's most popular fast-food chain, Happy Burger was busy on that beautiful Saturday afternoon. Not only were all the tables taken, but the queues for service were over ten people deep as well.

There was even a party going on in one corner of the room. Happy Harry, the Happy Burger Rabbit, was dancing around a clump of tables decorated with pink and green balloons, singing "Happy Birthday" at the top of his lungs. Happy Harry was six feet tall and a very warm shade of yellow. On occasions such as this he always wore a bright green foil hat that said "Happy Burgerday" in pink glitter across the front.

"It'll take Allie and Gemma hours to find us in here," Lizzie gloated as she and Charley fought their way to the counter at the back of the crowded room.

Charley, however, had stopped worrying about Allie, Gemma, and Mrs Moscos the second they stepped through the door.

"I wonder what I should have…" she mused. Happy Burger was her favourite restaurant. "I suppose I could just get a milkshake and some chips."

The overhead lights flickered as the girls finally came to a stop at the back of a queue. "You'll be lucky to get anything before midnight," said Lizzie. "There must be over a hundred people ahead of us."

But Charley wasn't looking at the long lines of customers, shuffling impatiently as they waited to order. She was looking at the menu on the wall.

"On the other hand," said Charley, "I didn't really have that much lunch. Maybe I'll get a burger, too."

"I wonder what's taking so long," said Lizzie. "I've never seen it as slow as this. Maybe they have a lot of new staff or something."

"But then again," Charley continued, "it's almost time for supper. Maybe I'll have a tea and one of those fruit pies so I don't spoil my appetite."

Lizzie stood on her toes, peering through the throng at the people behind the tills. They all wore pink and green uniforms and floppy green hats, a large plastic name tag that said "Happy Burgerday", and cheerful Happy Burger smiles.

"It's funny…" said Lizzie, "but I don't recognize anybody working here, and we come all the time."

Charley continued to gaze at the menu. "My father says they change staff a lot in places like this because the wages are so low," she answered absentmindedly.

Lizzie frowned. It wasn't just that she didn't recognize anyone. It was the people themselves. Usually, the Happy Burger workers bustled back and forth as swiftly and smoothly as robots, but today they all moved cautiously and awkwardly as though their shoes didn't fit. They had trouble punching orders into the computer; they picked up the wrong burgers and had difficulty closing the boxes; they scooped too many times to fill the chip cups; they let the drinks overflow.

Lizzie opened her mouth to mention this to Charley, but Charley was talking again.

"Of course," she was saying, "I could always have the frozen yoghurt…"

There was no point trying to talk to Charley when her stomach was in charge. Lizzie's attention wandered. Her eyes moved slowly round the room. The boy trying to sweep the floor with the wrong end of the broom wasn't familiar. The girl struggling to close the black bin liner wasn't familiar. The man who was stacking the trays the wrong way wasn't familiar, either.

Suddenly she saw someone who was. Two

someones. And *too* familiar. Allie and Gemma were coming through the door, carrier bags hanging from their arms like apples from a tree. Gemma said something to Allie. They both glanced back at the Kosmickicks sign on the other side of the shopping centre. Then they both started to laugh.

Lizzie could feel her face flush with anger. She'd been right! Allie and Gemma weren't worried about her and Charley. They were making them wait on purpose! They'd been buying half the shopping centre for the last hour, and now they were getting something to eat! Lizzie's lips formed a firm, straight line. There was no way she was going to let Allie and Gemma see them now. Her sister was really going to suffer this time.

"Forget the yoghurt," Lizzie hissed. "The Gruesome Twosome have just come in. We have to get out of here, quick!"

"But..." bleated Charley.

"No buts," said Lizzie grimly. "There's a

ladies downstairs. We can hide there. Come on, let's go." The lights flickered again. Lizzie glanced hopefully at the ceiling. If they went out completely, Allie would never be able to see them.

"But they're going to find us in the end," Charley reasoned. "At least let me get something to eat first."

"You can eat later," said Lizzie. "Allie hasn't had time to really suffer yet."

Lizzie pushed open the green and pink door to the Happy Burger ladies room and cautiously poked in her head. There was no one washing at the pink sinks; no feet showing beneath the green stalls.

"The coast is clear," she called. "Hurry!"

Charley followed her in, grumbling. "This is ridiculous, Allie's not even looking for us."

Lizzie grinned. For once in her life, she'd thought of everything.

"No, but she will be," said Lizzie. "And they'll be down here as soon as they've eaten

-32-

to check their make-up. And Allie can look, but she isn't going to find us." Lizzie headed for the nearest cubicle.

Charley trailed after her, her hands on her hips. "Oh, yeah? How can you be so sure?"

Lizzie opened the green metal door to reveal the pink toilet bowl. "Because we're going to lock ourselves in the toilets and keep our feet off the ground." It was a trick she'd seen in a film.

But Charley hadn't seen that film. Her hands stayed on her hips.

Lizzie gave her a shove. "Get in there, before Allie and Gemma turn up."

Obeying her own instructions, Lizzie bolted into the first cubicle and locked the door. Gingerly, she sat down on the seat and pressed her feet against the partition that separated her from Charley.

"All we have to do now is wait," she whispered, sounding pleased with herself.

The lights flickered again. And again.

The lights went out.

Charley moaned. "Yeah," she said. "All we have to do is wait."

"If you ask me, we're the ones who are suffering, not Allie and Gemma," Charley whispered through the partition. "We're down here, hiding like criminals, and they're upstairs, eating burgers and chips."

"At least the lights have come back on," said Lizzie.

"Big deal," grumbled Charley. "We've been here for ages. My legs and my bum are going numb."

Lizzie's legs and bum were going numb too. She looked at her watch to see how long they had been squashed up in the toilet.

"That can't be right. My watch must have stopped. What time do you make it?"

Charley answered immediately. "Ten past five." She must have been looking at her watch, too.

"That's what I make it," Lizzie put her watch to her ear. It was ticking away.

"Because that's what it is," said Charley.

"But it can't be," insisted Lizzie. "I looked at my watch when we came in here, and it was nearly ten past five then."

"You're confused," said Charley, sounding confused herself. "You must have made a mistake."

But Lizzie was certain. "We waited by the fountain till gone five. Then we waited in the queue for a few minutes, and it took us a couple of minutes to get down here..."

"I'm coming out," Charley suddenly announced.

Lizzie didn't argue. Instead, she stopped counting and got to her feet.

Lizzie and Charley stood side-by-side in front of the sinks, staring at their watches. It was still ten past five.

"See?" said Charley. "That's the answer. They must have stopped."

"But mine hasn't stopped." Lizzie held her watch to Charley's ear, at the same time as she put Charley's watch to her ear. Charley's watch was ticking too.

"The hands must be stuck," said Charley.

Lizzie was about to say it was unlikely the hands of both their watches should get stuck at the same time when something else caught her attention.

"Listen!" she hissed. "Do you hear what I hear?"

Charley blinked. "I don't hear anything, I'm still trying to work out what happened to our watches."

"Exactly," said Lizzie. "You don't hear anything."

Charley raised one eyebrow. "So?"

"So," said Lizzie, "where's the music?"

"Maybe you can't hear it down here," suggested Charley.

Lizzie made a disbelieving face. "You can *always* hear it. And besides, it isn't just the silence. It's the *sort* of silence."

Charley looked into Lizzie's eyes. "You mean like everything's been turned off?"

Lizzie nodded. "I think we should go up

and see what's happening." She really didn't like the silence. There was something unnatural about it. And anyway, it could be as late as five-thirty. Allie had probably been punished enough.

Hand-in-hand, Lizzie and Charley tiptoed up the stairs then stopped when they came to the pink and green door that led into the dining area. They leaned their ears against it.

"Nothing," whispered Charley. "I don't hear anything. Not even one kid screaming."

"On the count of three," said Lizzie. She closed her eyes. "Please," she said softly, "please don't let Allie be standing on the other side of this door." She opened her eyes again. "One..."

"Two..."

"Three..."

They pushed open the door.

"Gosh..." breathed Charlie.

"Wow..." said Lizzie.

* ★ ★

At least now they knew why they hadn't been able to hear anything. There was no one there. The restaurant was completely, eerily empty. Although there were meals on almost every table – some untouched, some half-eaten, some finished – there wasn't a single person anywhere in sight. The balloons at the party tables floated over empty chairs.

"Maybe there's been some kind of fire drill," suggested Lizzie.

"Yes," said Charley hopefully. "When we have fire drills at school everybody –" She broke off suddenly. "Is it me, or does everything look sort of *weird*?"

Lizzie had been thinking that very thing. "Look at the windows," she whispered back, pointing towards the far side of the room.

"Good grief," said Charley, "someone's painted them blue!"

Have a Nice Day!

....

"I told you we shouldn't have come here,"
Charley grumbled. Her voice echoed in the
empty room. "I told you we should have
listened to Mrs Moscos."

Lizzie scowled. Trust Charley to start
blaming *her* right away. "I don't remember
you telling me any such thing," she snapped.
"All I remember you doing is trying to decide
what to eat."

"That was *after* you made me come in
here." Charley waved her hands in the air.
"Look at this place," she wailed. "It's like the
Mary Celeste. It gives me the creeps."

"The *Mary Celeste*?" repeated Lizzie.
"Wasn't the *Mary Celeste* some sunken ship?"

Charley nodded solemnly. "No one ever
knew what happened to it. When they found
the ship there weren't any bodies, and

everything was left as though the people on board had been beamed up to another planet or something." She gestured to the tables cluttered with trays and food. "Just like here."

Lizzie stared at the table in front of them. There were two trays, each of them loaded with unopened burgers, full milkshakes and untouched chips. It looked as though someone had put them down and then gone back for ketchup. It gave her the creeps, too.

She pulled herself together with a shake. "Oh, please … I'm sure there's a perfectly reasonable explanation – I mean, we're in Happy Burger, Charley. Nothing bad happens here."

"Well…" Charley hesitated, willing to be convinced.

"No, really," Lizzie persisted, "I think you were right. I think there was a fire drill while we were in the ladies."

"So what about the blue, then?" asked Charley.

Reluctantly, Lizzie looked over at the windows and door. For some reason the blue was a little harder to explain than the sudden disappearance of hundreds of hamburger eaters had been.

"Maybe it's something they spray on the windows when there's a fire," Lizzie suggested. "To stop them from melting or something."

"You really think so?" Charley sounded relieved.

Lizzie nodded. A fire drill made sense to her. She felt pretty proud of herself for working it out.

"What do we do now?" asked Charley. Her voice was slightly muffled.

Lizzie was too busy staring at the door and windows to pay any attention to Charley's voice. The blue was moving ever so gently back and forth. "Charley," said Lizzie very softly. "Charley, I don't think the blue is paint after all. I think it must be some kind of cover." She chewed her bottom lip. "I saw this film once," she went on, thinking aloud. "There was a bomb in this building, so they covered the whole towerblock with this special material until the bomb squad could get there and defuse it."

"I saw it too," said Charley excitedly. "But how on earth could Mrs Moscos know someone was going to blow up Happy Burger? Unless…"

"Unless she's a terrorist," finished Lizzie. This, too, made sense. Mrs Moscos did come from Eastern Europe, after all. Lizzie knew from the news that there were quite a few terrorists in Eastern Europe. *And* Mrs Moscos was very odd…

"Gosh … a real terrorist!" Charley's voice sounded muffled again.

This time, Lizzie turned round. "Charlene Desoto!" she shrieked. "What are you doing?"

Charley looked down at the burger in her hand as though she wasn't sure how it came to be there. "I'm having a snack, that's what I'm doing."

"At a time like *this*?"

"Why not?" Charley demanded. "I mean, there's all this food just sitting here… Besides, I'm upset. Being upset makes me hungry."

"Well, being upset makes me want to leave," said Lizzie, already on her feet and heading towards the entrance. "I think we should get out of here. Now."

Charley's chair scraped against the floor as she hurried after Lizzie.

"Wait for me!" cried Charley. "Don't leave me by myself!"

Lizzie reached for the door handle and pulled. Nothing happened.

Charley's head appeared over Lizzie's shoulder. "What's wrong?"

Lizzie gave another yank. "I can't open it. It must be stuck."

"It is not stuck," said a voice behind them. "It is locked hard."

Lizzie and Charley collided in their hurry to turn round.

Standing behind one of the tills was a small, round woman almost as wide as she was tall. She was wearing the pink and green Happy Burger uniform. Her floppy hat was set on her head at a dangerous angle, and there was a plastic tag that said, "Hello! My name is Mischka. Have a Nice Day!" pinned to her chest.

"Mrs Moscos?" gasped Lizzie. "Mrs Moscos, what are you doing here?"

"I might be asking you the very same thing," said Mrs Moscos.

Charley, who had been staring at Mrs Moscos in something of a stunned silence, suddenly spoke.

"Good grief," said Charley. "It *is* Mrs Moscos." She turned to Lizzie. "What's Mrs Moscos doing here?" she demanded.

"Well, I am not placing bombs in the deep fryer, I will tell you that," said Mrs Moscos stiffly. "I am working under the covers. Today I am saving the world."

Small, nervous smiles appeared on the

faces of the girls.

"Saving the world?" asked Lizzie. "You're saving the world from Happy Burger?"

"Of course not." Mrs Moscos smiled sourly. "It is much too late for that. I am saving the world from Wei."

"Why?" repeated Lizzie.

Mrs Moscos, however, thought she was asking a question. "Because someone has to," said Mrs Moscos.

Mrs Moscos Explains What Wei Is and One or Two Other Little Things

....

"You're confusing us, Mrs Moscos," said Lizzie patiently. "Who is Wei, and why do you have to save the world from him?"

Mrs Moscos came out from behind the counter and strode across the room. "Wei is not a who," she said in a tone that suggested that this should have been obvious. She reached past them for the door.

"It won't open," said Lizzie. "Remember? You said it was locked."

"Locked to you," said Mrs Moscos. The door swung back silently.

Charley gave Lizzie a look. She'd never seen anyone open a locked door without a key before.

Lizzie gazed at the small, stocky figure in the pink and green uniform. She'd always known there was something strange about Mrs Moscos, but she'd had no idea just how strange.

"How did you do that?" Lizzie demanded.

"Let's have less questions and more action," said Mrs Moscos crisply. "We have a very busy afternoon ahead of us. Now, Lizzie, please will you hold the door for a second?"

Still attached to Charley, who wasn't about to loosen her grip, Lizzie took hold of the door. Now she could see that the material surrounding Happy Burger was a little like parachute silk and a little like aluminium foil.

Without another word, Mrs Moscos ran a finger down it and it opened as though she had cut it. The temperature immediately dropped by at least forty degrees. A gust of wind blew the cloth apart.

"Lizzie," Charley hissed. "Lizzie, that's *not* the shopping centre out there."

Lizzie was too shocked to do more than nod. It certainly wasn't the shopping centre. Instead of the fountain and the shops, and the bickering families, a barren landscape of black rocks and silver soil stretched before them as far as the eye could see. Dust storms of gold, green and copper swirled across the ground; magenta clouds blotted out the sun and sky.

Mrs Moscos removed a small black and silver object from her bag. It looked like the kind of mask cyclists use to avoid being poisoned by traffic pollution. "Of course it's not the shopping centre." Mrs Moscos clamped the mask over her mouth and nose and stepped lightly through the opening. "This," she announced, spreading her arms as though embracing the dusty gloom, "is the great planet Wei."

"Planet?" gasped Lizzie, suddenly aware that she was having some difficulty breathing. She wasn't sure what she'd been expecting to hear, but she was fairly certain that that wasn't it.

"You never heard of it?" asked Mrs Moscos. "It's very famous." She winked. "Or should I say 'infamous'?"

"Are you saying we're on another planet?" asked Lizzie. "One that isn't the Earth?"

Charley let out a low moan. "Another planet?" She turned on Lizzie, her lower lip trembling. "Look at the mess you've got us into," she wailed. "Now we'll *never* get home in time."

Mrs Moscos shrugged. "You should have thought of that before you went into Happy Burger." She turned to Lizzie. "I did tell you not to, didn't I? I think I was quite clear."

Lizzie glared back at Charley and Mrs Moscos. It really was too much the way everyone always blamed her for everything.

"But you didn't say *why*," protested Lizzie. "If you'd told me why…"

"And did you ask?" Mrs Moscos removed the mask from her face and marched back into the restaurant. "Not that it matters. What would you have done if I had told you you shouldn't go into the Happy Burger because it was going to be transported to Wei?" she demanded. "Would you have said,

'Thank you very much, Mrs Moscos. Charley and I will be certain to keep away'?"

Even Lizzie had to admit to herself that this seemed a little improbable. But no more improbable than being beamed up to some distant galaxy.

"Maybe … I—" started Lizzie.

"I do not think so," interrupted Mrs Moscos. "You would have thought I was making up a story and done exactly what you did do." She arched one eyebrow. "Which was to pay no attention to what I said at all."

"You can't prove that," said Lizzie stubbornly, ignoring the fact that Charley was nodding her head in agreement.

"I do not have to." Mrs Moscos ran her finger down the opening and the blue cloth sealed itself shut. "Knowledge is not always dependent on proof."

"It really is fascinating how the universe likes to repeat itself," Mrs Moscos informed them as she placed three paper cups on the table.

"Take Wei, for example. It is quite similar to the Earth in many ways."

"No, it isn't," said Lizzie. Not only was she still in shock, but she was also still smarting from being blamed for everything. She wasn't going to agree with anything Mrs Moscos said without an argument. "It's cold and cloudy and there aren't any trees or plants…"

Charley sniffed at her cup. "What is this?" she wanted to know. "It looks like water." The only time Charley drank water was when she took her daily vitamins.

"It *is* water," said Mrs Moscos. Seeing the doubt on Charley's face, she added, "It's all right to drink. You're not on the Earth, remember. The water's safe." Mrs Moscos turned back to Lizzie. "Those are minor details," she informed her coolly. She waved one hand as though brushing those minor details aside. "It is always cloudy, so there is no real sunlight, and there is no real sunlight, so nothing grows and it is always cold."

"But what about the animals?" countered

Lizzie. Her class was studying food chains in science. "How can they live if there aren't any plants?"

Mrs Moscos shook her head. "There aren't any animals on Wei. On Wei there are only Weis. And you and I, of course."

"I bet there isn't any public transport, either," said Charley glumly.

"Not any that goes to Meteor Drive," said Mrs Moscos. "Though you might catch a ride to within three or four galaxies of the Milky Way." She smiled as though this was good news.

"But how do they breathe?" asked Lizzie. "If there aren't any plants, there isn't any oxygen–"

"That is not a problem," said Mrs Moscos. "If you travel through the atmosphere of Wei, you use a POT."

Lizzie and Charley exchanged a look. What good was a pot when you couldn't breathe? "A pot?" they asked together.

Mrs Moscos pointed to the black and silver

mask she'd been wearing earlier. "This," she informed them, "is a POT. A personal oxygen tank. It makes breathing very easy." She held up one hand. "Now, if you would give me a chance, I might perhaps explain."

Once the planet Wei was even more like the Earth, Mrs Moscos told them. It had plants, and weather, and animals, and trees. It had rivers and lakes, and sunny days. But the Weis were greedy. Instead of taking care of their planet, they slowly destroyed it. They killed the animals. They chopped down the forests. They came very close to making themselves extinct. Now the Weis lived in enormous domed eco-cities. These cities manufactured their own electricity, food and water, and were topped by forests that grew above the cloud line and allowed the Weis to continue to breathe. Since there wasn't much on Wei worth visiting, the Weis rarely left their cities unless it was to go somewhere else. Which, because their planet was both uninteresting and inhospitable, they apparently did quite a lot.

"Weis are the great explorers of the cosmos," said Mrs Moscos. "You can hardly move an inch through time and space without tripping over a Wei."

"Well, I've never seen one," snapped Lizzie.

Mrs Moscos gave her a look. "Oh, but you have, Lizzie Wesson. You have seen quite a few Weis, as it happens."

Even Charley stopped worrying about getting a bus home at this information. "Really?" she asked. "Where?"

"Why, right here!" Mrs Moscos gestured. "Taking the orders … making the food … clearing the trays…"

Lizzie was willing to believe most of Mrs Moscos's story because of the simple fact that they obviously were on another planet, but this, she felt, was going too far.

"Oh, come on, Mrs Moscos," said Lizzie. "I think Charley and I would have known if we were being served by aliens disguised as Happy Burger employees."

"Oh, do you?" Mrs Moscos arched her eyebrows. "Firstly, my young friend, I think it would be good for you to remember that, on this planet, you and Charley are the aliens." She lifted her cup and took a sip. "Secondly, Weis do not have three eyes or pointy cars. They have evolved very much like humans and, as they've been visiting the Earth since the ice melted, quite a few Weis are part human as well. Superficially, they are identical."

Lizzie gave in reluctantly. "I did notice that the Happy Burger employees had trouble walking," she admitted.

"Trainers," said Mrs Moscos simply. "They're used to wearing space boots."

"And they don't seem very good at running a restaurant," Lizzie went on.

"The Weis are very advanced," said Mrs Moscos. "They aren't used to manual labour any more. They think things rather than do them." Noticing the blank looks she was getting from her companions, Mrs Moscos explained. "If a Wei wants to open a door, it will think the door open rather than use the handle."

Lizzie frowned. "You mean they *thought* the Happy Burger here?"

Mrs Moscos's laughter echoed through the empty room. "No, no, no. Space-time travel is a little more complicated than that."

Charley cleared her throat. "I don't understand, Mrs Moscos. Why did the Weis bring us to Wei?"

"I'm coming to that." Mrs Moscos finished her water and began to explain.

The ruler of the Weis was Louis Zu. Louis Zu was very fond of the planet Earth. It was his favourite place to visit. There was so much to see, so much to do. But what Louis Zu liked best of all about the Earth were hamburgers, television, and Disneyland. Louis Zu was mad about Disneyland.

"And because he is so fond of the Earth," concluded Mrs Moscos, "he naturally wants to own it."

"Own it?" Lizzie was still frowning. "How can he own the Earth by kidnapping a Happy Burger?"

Mrs Moscos tapped her temple with one finger. "He is a very clever Wei, Louis Zu. Even I have to admit that it is a brilliant plan. Truly inspired." She smiled almost triumphantly. "He's going to take over your planet through the Happy Burger chain. After all, it does cover the entire globe."

Charley glanced at the burger she'd been eating earlier. "You mean by poisoning the food?" she asked nervously.

Mrs Moscos laughed again. "Oh, I don't think there's any need for that," she said and went on with her story.

The reason Louis Zu transported the Victoria Shopping Centre's Happy Burger to Wei was because he needed a model. He was going to copy the Happy Burger down to the most minute detail. Then he was going to make thousands, maybe millions of them. Only they wouldn't be fast-food restaurants.

They would be fully armed Wei warships. When they were ready, they would land on the Earth. Most would merely replace real restaurants. But in the rare places in the world that didn't have a Happy Burger every few hundred feet, they would be set down in strategic locations. And then, naturally, the rest would be simple. The combined strength of every army, navy and airforce on the planet wouldn't be enough to thwart a surprise attack of that magnitude by the Weis. The Earth and everything on it would be theirs within seconds.

"Gosh," said Charley. "What's he going to do with the Earth when he gets it? Use it as a military base?"

Mrs Moscos shook her head. "No, no, no. Your planet is useless for anything like that. He's going to turn it into an intergalactic theme park." She smiled wryly. "It's very clever, isn't it? He will already have all the restaurants he needs."

An intergalactic theme park! Lizzie's

parents wouldn't like that very much. They protested every time the council wanted to build another road.

"And you're going to stop him?" asked Lizzie, feeling a little awed. This wasn't the sort of behaviour you expected from a middle-aged woman, not even one from Eastern Europe.

"Not I," corrected Mrs Moscos. "We."

Lizzie and Charley looked at each other. "We?"

"Yes," said Mrs Moscos. "You and I – we – are going to stop the Weis."

One or Two Things Mrs Moscos Forgot to Tell Lizzie and Charley

....

Having finished both her water and her explanation, Mrs Moscos got to her feet.

"There is a lot to do," she informed them briskly. "And the first thing we must attend to is getting ourselves out of here." She tilted her head towards the entrance and the Happy Burger hat slipped over her eyes. Looking a little annoyed, Mrs Moscos took it off and stuffed it in her yellow canvas bag. "They will be putting guards around the building very soon, and we don't want to be here when they arrive."

Charley choked on her water. "Guards? With guns?"

Mrs Moscos started removing her uniform. Underneath she was wearing the baggy jeans and Greenpeace T-shirt she usually wore when she did her shopping.

"Oh, there will certainly be gun
Moscos assured her. "Weis are ver
guns. I mentioned that they are ve.... ...
humans, didn't I?"

Lizzie looked at Charley. Somehow, the
thought that the Weis were so human wasn't
as comforting as it should be.

Mrs Moscos put the Happy Burger
uniform in her yellow bag, and took out
something silver and shimmering at the same
time. "So," she said, neatly stepping into
what looked rather like designer mechanics'
overalls, "now we will be on our way."

"Where are we going?" asked Charley,
making no attempt to hide her terror.

Mrs Moscos paid no attention to the fear
in Charley's voice.

"To Yurn," she said, "the capital of the
Wei Empire, and the largest eco-city in the
universe. If we are to save the Earth, we must
get into Louis Zu's headquarters and find the
transporter he is using for this project."

She smiled thinly. "You understand, of course, that Louis Zu did not construct this transporter himself. It is much too sophisticated for Wei technology." She shook her head sadly but sternly. "No, Louis Zu stole the transporter. His scientists won't be able to construct another for at least a thousand of your years. That isn't that long a time on Wei, but on the Earth it is. By then, with a little luck, your species will be over its obsession with fast food, so he'll have to come up with another plan. Therefore, it is our job to de-transport the restaurant before he can replicate it. But before we can do that, we must also rescue the others."

"The others?" squeaked Lizzie. What with the shock of finding Mrs Moscos and everything, she'd forgotten about the others.

"What did you think?" enquired Mrs Moscos. "You must have realized that they'd been transported, just as you were. After all, you knew enough to hide downstairs during the journey, didn't you?"

So that was why their watches stopped and the lights went out. They'd been hurtling through space and time. Lizzie couldn't help feeling a little pleased at her cleverness, even though it was accidental. She smiled at Charley and Mrs Moscos. "That's right," she said. "I did, didn't I?"

"We were hiding from your sister, not the Weis," Charley reminded her.

"The reason does not matter to the cosmos," said Mrs Moscos. "The important thing is that you would have been given transportation gas like the others if you had stayed up the stairs. By now you would be imprisoned in Yurn."

"Transportation gas?" Lizzie had once had gas at the dentist's. She didn't like it at all.

"It is used very much for space-time travel," Mrs Moscos explained. "Especially if you are transporting creatures who do not know that they are being moved. In the first stage, the creature is in a deep trance, unaware of anything. In the second, he or she is in a time bubble, repeating the ten minutes before they were transported over and over again. As you will have guessed, this means that *if* they ever return to their own planet, they will not remember a thing."

"What do you mean *if*?" asked the two girls at once.

"Oh, didn't I mention?" Mrs Moscos swung her yellow bag over her shoulder. "Louis Zu will need the Happy Burger employees and customers to train the Weis. The Weis will watch them do the same tasks and say the same things over and over again. They'll learn how to speak to one another as if they were human. They'll be able to imitate them down to their finest detail."

"And what'll happen to the humans once the Weis know everything there is to know about working in Happy Burger?" asked Lizzie warily.

Mrs Moscos shrugged. "After the Happy Burger is useful as a model, Louis Zu will add it to his private collection of zoos."

The girls exchanged horrified looks.

"You mean, instead of elephants in cages eating hay, there'll be people eating hamburgers?" gasped Charley.

Mrs Moscos nodded as though there was nothing bizarre about this at all.

"Louis is famous for his zoos," she informed them. "He's been collecting specimens from every universe for thousands of your years. But this is the first time he will have one with creatures in their natural habitat." She started walking to the back of the room. "Now, come on, girls. For once do as you are told. We do not have time that can be thrown away."

"But I don't *want* to help stop Louis Zu," Charley protested softly as she and Lizzie followed Mrs Moscos through the silent Happy Burger kitchen. "I want to go home."

Lizzie wouldn't have minded going home, but on the other hand she rather liked the idea of stopping Louis Zu. She turned to

Charley. "Well, we can't go home," she whispered back. "And if we don't help Mrs Moscos we may be stuck here for ever."

Charley folded her arms in front of her. "This is all your fault, Lizzie Wesson. If you'd listened to Mrs Moscos in the first place, we'd be home right now, having tea."

"Well, we're not," Lizzie growled. "And there's no way we're ever going to leave if we don't stop the Weis." A tiny smile appeared on her face. The idea of saving the Earth and being a hero rather appealed to Lizzie. Even her parents wouldn't punish a hero for getting home late. She leaned closer to Charley. "Maybe you don't mind spending the rest of your life in a zoo, but I do."

"Isn't there one tiny thing you've forgotten?" Charley asked sourly. "What if we get caught trying to rescue the others? They won't put us in the zoo..." She paused dramatically. "They'll put us in the cemetery."

Lizzie stared at Charley in silence. Oddly

enough, the idea that they might be captured hadn't occurred to her. She'd imagined herself leading a group of dazed but grateful shoppers to safety; she hadn't imagined being caught by angry Wei guards. Lizzie decided that being captured was something it might be better not to think about.

"We won't get caught," she said confidently. "We're with Mrs Moscos."

"Mrs Moscos!" Charley's eyes widened in alarm. "Lizzie, Mrs Moscos's gone!"

Lizzie looked around. There was no one else in the kitchen.

"Come on!" She grabbed Charley's hand. "She must have gone through the back door."

They raced towards the green door with the Exit sign over it. Mrs Moscos looked like a harmless, middle-aged woman from Eastern Europe in much the same way that Clark Kent looked like a mild-mannered reporter. But underneath she was a Cosmic Avenger … an Intergalactic Superspy … a Warrior of the Stars. Without Mrs Moscos,

Lizzie and Charley were sitting ducks.

Her heart pounding, Lizzie yanked open the exit door to reveal a small garage. In the middle of the garage, a green golf cart with pink and green awnings trembled slightly as its engine warmed up.

"Wow!" gasped Lizzie. "It's the Happy Burgermobile!"

The Happy Burgermobile was usually driven by Happy Harry, the Happy Burger Rabbit. Today, however, Harry was not behind the wheel. Behind the pink and green steering wheel was Mrs Moscos. She was wearing what looked like a purple motorcycle helmet with a tinted visor.

"Who's she going to save us from?" hissed Charley. "Ronald McDonald?"

Lizzie gripped the bar that supported the roof, and Charley gripped Lizzie as the gaudily painted golf cart slowly made its way through the dust storms and black hills of Wei. It was difficult to see clearly because of the goggles, the straw hats, and the POTS Mrs Moscos had insisted they wear, but far in the distance, Lizzie could just make out the glass dome that enveloped Yurn, glinting like a bubble against the magenta sky. A shiver ran through her. She, Lizzie Wesson of 34 Meteor Drive, was about to enter the capital city of an alien empire! Lizzie was no longer bothered that she hadn't bought a new top. What did that matter? She was about to become a hero. Beside her Charley shifted unhappily.

"Mrs Moscos," said Charley in her most polite voice. "If you don't mind my saying so, I don't think this is going to work."

The little pink and green cart bounced as it hit a dip. Silver soil spilled around them like stars.

"And why would I mind you saying that?" inquired Mrs Moscos. "It is not true."

Charley cleared her throat. "Well, a Happy Burgermobile isn't exactly inconspicuous, is it?"

Mrs Moscos glanced over at Charley while

narrowly missing another deep dip.

"Unlike little girls, this car does not have to be inconspicuous," she replied evenly. "By now all of Wei knows that the Happy Burger has landed. And everyone will also know that this is the car of famous Harry the Rabbit. He is something of a hero on Wei."

Charley frowned.

Lizzie leaned across Charley to gawp at Mrs Moscos.

"Happy Harry?" asked Lizzie in shock. "Happy Harry's a hero on Wei?"

It wasn't easy to imagine Happy Harry with his hat and his pink and green balloons as a hero anywhere, much less on another planet. Lizzie had never imagined that other planets might be into giant singing rabbits.

"Television," said Mrs Moscos. "Weis love your adverts. And Louis Zu is especially fond of Harry. He has a poster of him on the wall of his office." She wiped dust from the visor of her helmet. "Life-size," she added.

"I don't see how that helps us," said Charley.

Mrs Moscos shook her head in disappointment. "I was right about you two shopping too much. Shopping does not encourage thinking."

She revved the engine as they came to a steep slope. "It is simple, really. Louis Zu loves Harry, and everything connected with Harry. Since Louis Zu loves the Happy Burgermobile, Louis Zu must, of course, have it." Mrs Moscos smiled. "And we are bringing it to him."

"We are?" Lizzie felt something very cold and damp run down her spine. She'd assumed that they were going to sneak into Yurn, not drive in in the Happy Burgermobile. She could only hope that, like Clark Kent, Mrs Moscos had some special powers that she was keeping hidden.

"You see this uniform I am wearing?" asked Mrs Moscos.

Lizzie and Charley looked first at each other, and then at the silver overalls. "Yeah."

"This is the uniform of the Jits, Louis Zu's

personal army. With it, I can get into Louis Zu's headquarters, take the transporter and discover where the other humans are being kept. All I have to do is say that I am on a special mission to bring the Happy Burgermobile directly to him, and the gates will open wide." She tapped the rectangle of plastic that was pinned to the pocket of her overalls. "See? I have an official I.D. card and everything." Her expression became stern. "All that is asked of you two is to look straight ahead and be very still. Pretend you are the dummies in the store window. And remember, only walk if someone is leading you. Otherwise just stand where you are as though you're made out of plastic and modelling clothes."

"But why?" Acting like a dummy didn't seem very heroic to Lizzie. What was she going to say when the newspapers asked her what part she played in saving the world? *I kept my mouth shut?*

Mrs Moscos heaved a heavy sigh. "Because

although you look like Weis, they will smell you are human. The crisps, the chips, the chocolate bars … the smell is unmistakable. So they must believe that you have had the transportation gas like the others, but that somehow you were left behind when they moved the humans from the restaurant."

Charley looked confused. "But what about you, Mrs Moscos? Won't they smell you?"

Mrs Moscos heaved another, even heavier, sigh. "It is true that I am a naturalized citizen of the United Kingdom," she said patiently, "but that does not mean that I am of human birth."

Lizzie leaned forward again to stare at her next-door neighbour. Somehow, even though Mrs Moscos had been doing some pretty strange things today, it hadn't occurred to Lizzie to wonder where she was really from.

"You mean you're a Wei?" she asked excitedly. Just wait till her parents heard about this!

"No," said Mrs Moscos, all of a sudden

sounding cold and vague. "That is not what I mean. As it occurs, I like to think of myself as a citizen of the cosmos."

A citizen of the cosmos… The words echoed in Lizzie's head as they ploughed through the shimmering dust of Wei. *A citizen of the cosmos.* She liked the sound of that. Now that she was going to help save the world, maybe she could consider herself a citizen of the cosmos, too. Lizzie smiled at the thought. Lizzie Wesson – citizen of the cosmos. She liked the sound of that, too.

Mrs Moscos's
Sense of Humour

....

"Pinch me," ordered Lizzie in a whisper.
"Pinch me so I know I'm not dreaming."
Though, how could she be dreaming? Lizzie's
dreams were about things like turning up for
school in her pyjamas or being given a
hundred pounds to spend as she wanted.
They were nothing like this.

Sprawling across the silver soil for miles in
front of them was the great eco-city of Yurn,
capital of the mighty Wei Empire. Its silver
towers disappeared into the clouds. Its blue-
white lights shone like trillions of stars. And
covering it all was a dome of spun glass,
which made Yurn look as though it were
embedded in ice.

"It's incredible!" Charley's voice was softer
than a breath.

"It sure beats the shopping centre," agreed

Lizzie. The shopping centre and any other place she had ever seen. Even Disneyland.

"It must be bigger than Europe," said Charley as they drove into a swirling cone of copper dust.

Lizzie's enthusiasm for becoming a hero faltered slightly. How were they ever going to find the other humans in a city that was bigger than Europe?

But there wasn't any time to worry about that. Just ahead of them, the entrance to Yurn appeared on the other side of the copper haze. Standing with their backs to the gates were a dozen guards in black armour and silver capes. They all carried guns.

Charley's fingers dug into Lizzie's arm. "Look at those guards," she hissed. "They must be friends of Darth Vadar."

"They look more like very close relatives, if you ask me," whispered Lizzie.

"No more talking," snapped Mrs Moscos. "Remember, you are in a trance. Eyes open, but minds empty." She glanced over. "That shouldn't be too hard," she added unkindly.

And with that the Happy Burgermobile screeched to a halt within inches of several pairs of highly polished boots.

Lizzie half expected the guards to start laughing at the sight of the dust-covered golf cart and the two of them in their hats and goggles. Either laugh or shoot them. But the guards drew themselves to attention and saluted smartly. It seemed incredible to Lizzie, since the Weis were supposed to be so advanced, but they actually believed Mrs Moscos was a Jit.

Mrs Moscos smartly returned their salute.

"Goulashfortea," said the guard – at least it sounded to Lizzie like goulashfortea.

"Jumblefishtoes," replied Mrs Moscos.

"Goonandwinewithantsunderhailstones."

Mrs Moscos nodded.

"Backwashorangecurtainsunduly."

The Wei language being both impenetrable and strangely melodic, Lizzie found it easy to pretend to be in a trance as she listened to

Mrs Moscos explain her mission to the guard. So successful was Lizzie in imitating a mannequin, in fact, that she almost forgot where she was. It was the smell of rotten eggs that brought her back to reality – or what was passing for reality at the moment.

The guard was scrutinizing her and Charley so closely that Lizzie had to do all she could not to gag. Weis certainly didn't smell like chocolate, crisps or chips. You're in a trance, you're in a trance... Lizzie silently repeated, desperately reminding herself how unpleasant life in a zoo would be.

"Mincetomtomoverbrickle," intoned the guard.

"Bullwhipsanddustbins," answered Mrs Moscos.

The guard spoke too quickly for Lizzie to hear more than sounds, but she could tell from the way he was pointing through the gates that he was going to let them pass.

"Berriesraininmudvarks," said Mrs Moscos.

The guard solemnly raised one gloved hand. The crystal gates slid silently apart, and, balloons bobbing, Mrs Moscos drove the Happy Burgermobile into the capital of the Wei Empire.

"You see," she said as the gates closed behind them, "Didn't I tell you we'd have no problems?"

Yurn was even more impressive close up than it was from a distance. From a distance, it was just another alien mega-eco-city. It wasn't until you were inside that you could see how magnificent it really was. The buildings were silver, and so tall that their tops couldn't be seen from the ground. The streets were wide and paved with glass that shimmered in the artificial sunlight. The air was still and pure, and slightly green from the wilderness growing on the roofs. Electricity hummed all around them, but there were no honking horns or alarms or screeching sirens. The only traffic was a few official cars and bullet-shaped silver buses, covered with thousands of tiny lights, that floated several inches above the ground. But there were pedestrians. The streets were crowded with Weis, all of them wearing the black and silver colours of the Empire.

Lizzie felt a shiver of excitement run through her. Yurn was the most incredible city she had ever seen or imagined.

"Gosh…" breathed Charley. "It's even better than Oz."

The Burgermobile stopped outside a windowless black skyscraper spangled with purple lights. It was the only building that wasn't silver, and the only one with guards at the entrance. Lizzie, who had been so fascinated with the city she'd almost forgotten why they were there, forced her attention back to the matter at hand.

"So what happens now, Mrs Moscos?" she asked softly. She was determined to do exactly as she was told, as a good hero should.

Mrs Moscos nodded towards the black skyscraper. "Now we enter Wei government headquarters," she replied very quietly. "You may take off your POTS, but please be good enough to keep on your hats and goggles."

Lizzie sighed. She'd assumed that they were going in; what she wanted to know was what they were going to do when they got there. Maybe Mrs Moscos didn't see any problems, but Lizzie did. How were they going to search the building for the other humans without anyone noticing? There were guards everywhere.

"Now, no more talking," warned Mrs Moscos, carefully guiding first Lizzie and then Charley out of the Burgermobile. She clapped a hand firmly on each of their shoulders.

Forbidden to speak, Lizzie thought about secret weapons. All heroes had secret weapons. What was Mrs Moscos's? Karate? Judo? A laser gun? The ability to make herself invisible? Being invisible had a lot to recommend it. Lizzie could think of quite a few advantages to being invisible in everyday life, but the advantages in Yurn could mean the difference between being a hero and being a prisoner of Louis Zu. The more Lizzie thought about it, the more it seemed to her that that had to be Mrs Moscos's secret weapon. Mrs Moscos could open and close things without touching them – surely she could make them vanish just as easily. Confidently waiting to disappear, Lizzie let Mrs Moscos lead her and Charley through the massive metal doors.

It was even brighter inside the black building than it was on the streets of Yurn. Sparkling silver and glass hallways stretched out in every direction. Official-looking Weis with serious expressions hurried past them, their footsteps ringing like chimes on the crystal floors.

Several Weis stopped to look at them, nudging each other and smiling. Mrs Moscos paid no attention. Seeming to know her way through the maze of corridors, she marched along with an air of purpose and authority.

A guard was posted at every intersection, but none of them did more than glance at Mrs Moscos's ID and nod them on.

Still thinking about becoming invisible, Lizzie was surprised to find herself being pushed into a large glass lift.

"You are doing much better than I would have imagined," Mrs Moscos praised them as the lift silently rose. "Perhaps so much shopping has had its benefits after all. At least you know how to act like dummies."

Lizzie barely heard. Her attention was caught by the lilac lights over the door that showed they had passed the fiftieth floor. They passed the hundredth. They sped past the second hundred, then the third.

Charley was also watching the progress of the lift. "Mrs Moscos," she ventured. "Mrs Moscos, I think I'm feeling a little air sick."

"No vomiting," ordered Mrs Moscos. "It is not the time. We are almost there."

At the sixth hundredth floor, the lift stopped. The doors opened on another glass and metal corridor. There was a solid silver door at the very end. Mrs Moscos shoved them out of the lift. Lizzie took a deep breath. Any second now, Mrs Moscos was going to snap her fingers and make them disappear.

The silver door slid open at their approach. Standing between them and an inner door was a guard in the same silver overalls and purple helmet as Mrs Moscos. She was slightly taller and slightly thinner than Mrs Moscos, but otherwise it was impossible to tell them apart.

A real Jit, thought Lizzie. That must mean they were close to Louis Zu.

"Sherpamaroons?" asked the guard crisply.

Lizzie clenched her teeth, bracing herself for the moment when Mrs Moscos did something fantastic.

"Yammermettleecocypherdaffodil," announced Mrs Moscos.

"Beansnobacon," replied the Jit.

Mrs Moscos reached into a pocket on her uniform and pulled out a postcard. Even from behind her goggles, Lizzie could see that it was a Happy Burger postcard. The bright photograph on the front showed Happy Harry skipping through Happy Burgerland, with a smiling child on either side of him holding his paws. Both children were wearing straw hats and goggles.

The guard took the card and studied it carefully.

"Louis Zu bumbleticklesundersheepshearer," said Mrs Moscos. She patted the shoulders she was holding. "Louis Zu mucklemumblestuff."

The Jit looked from the glossy postcard to Lizzie and Charley.

"Ripetideoverwappingbanger," said the Jit. And then she turned, walked through a wall that opened behind her, and disappeared.

Lizzie knew she wasn't supposed to talk, but the way events seemed to be going was worrying her slightly.

"Mrs Moscos," whispered Lizzie. "Mrs Moscos, was that supposed to be me and Charley on that postcard?"

"It's a misfortune that you are not as obedient as you are observant," said Mrs Moscos curtly.

"But was it?" insisted Lizzie.

"I told you," said Mrs Moscos, under her breath. "Louis Zu likes anything to do with Happy Harry. Now if it is not *too* much trouble, I would appreciate some silence. You are not two hundred metres from Louis Zu."

"But Mrs Moscos—" began Lizzie.

Mrs Moscos squeezed her shoulder tight. "Shhh!" she warned. "The guard is coming back."

The silver wall opened again.

"Milkweedmazelweeder Louis Zu," intoned the Jit. She stepped aside and gestured them forward.

A hand on each of their shoulders, Mrs Moscos marched Lizzie and Charley through the door. The next wall silently slid back. Then the next and the next. As they stepped through each opening, it closed behind them. At last they came to a wall as black as obsidian, which drew back slowly at their approach.

Lizzie forced herself not to gasp in astonishment. The room before them was miles high and the size of a football pitch. The walls, floor and ceiling were black, and the lighting had a faint tinge of blue. A multitude of tiny lights flashed and shone, a thousand circuits hummed. Banks of electronic equipment and computers sprawled across the central space. At least half of the dozen Weis in the room were Jit guards.

"Wow…" said Lizzie under her breath. She turned to see if Mrs Moscos was going to give them some indication of what was going to happen next.

But Mrs Moscos was no longer standing behind Lizzie and Charley with her hands on their shoulders. Mrs Moscos had finally done something fantastic.

She had totally disappeared.

Charley's hand closed around Lizzie's. Her

palm was damp with sweat.

"Where's she gone?" she whispered. There was so much electronic equipment around them and everyone seemed so busy that it wasn't likely any of the Weis would hear them even if they shouted.

"She could be anywhere," answered Lizzie, gesturing to the milling Jits. "All the guards look exactly alike."

But although she was talking about the Jits, Lizzie was staring past them. At the opposite side of the room, the wall was a TV screen that was bigger than any cinema screen Lizzie had ever seen. At the moment, it seemed to be showing a documentary on astronomy. There was something faintly familiar about the image of a black section of space dotted with thousands of pastel stars, but Lizzie had no time to think about it.

Facing the screen were half a dozen solemn-looking Weis in silver uniforms. In front of them, with his back to the others, was a tall, thin Wei all in black. His voice was shrill but powerful; his manner sure. He was a Wei who was used to being listened to and used to being obeyed. Lizzie guessed from the way he was gesturing that he was talking about the programme on the screen.

Whatever he was doing, the Weis were all so absorbed that none of them had noticed the sudden arrival in their midst of Lizzie Wesson and Charley Desoto.

"Good grief," breathed Charley. "What are they watching, *The Sky at Night*?"

Her eyes on the screen and the Wei in black, Lizzie shook her head very slightly. She'd just realized why the programme seemed so familiar. What she had taken for stars were actually pairs of minuscule pink and green balloons, bent towards each other to make a heart.

"Look," Lizzie whispered excitedly. "Those tiny dots are Happy Burgers!"

"And that black bit that looks like outer space is the Earth," Charley squeezed her hand even tighter. "Lizzie, do you know what that must mean?"

Lizzie knew what it must mean. It must mean that what they were looking at was not an educational documentary on the universe, but the Wei plans for taking over the Earth. Every pink and green dot marked the future location of an armed Wei warship. Or, if you looked at it another way, of a hamburger restaurant in the Planet Earth Theme Park.

Lizzie felt as though she'd fallen out of a spaceship, assuming, that is, that falling out of a spaceship sent your stomach down to your toes. If this was a map of the world, then she and Charley really were in Mission Control. Lizzie's heart picked up speed. If this was Mission Control, then the gentleman in black with the air of authority must be none other than Louis Zu himself.

Lizzie turned to Charley. Charley had figured it out, too. She was staring back at Lizzie with the identical look of horror on her face. But before either of them could say anything, the room suddenly became as still as a dead star.

Louis Zu had turned to face his audience. He was an impressive sight. He was slender, but he was straight and solid. His hair shone like silver and his eyes glowed gold. One hand was held high in the air. His regal head was raised and the hard mouth pursed.

"TipplethewashbogPLANETEARTH!"

The other Weis raised their heads and shouted back, "TipplethewashbogPLANET-EARTH!"

"HAPPYBURGER!" boomed Louis Zu. "Mintlinnetsmacaroni!"

The others raised their arms, too. "Mintlinnetsmacaroni!" they screamed.

Louis Zu raised his other hand and held them both high and wide. His voice rang through the enormous room. "THEME-PARK! HAPPYHARRY!"

"THEMEPARK! HAPPYHARRY!!" intoned the silver-suited Weis.

Suddenly overwhelmed with panic, Lizzie pulled Charley behind the nearest console.

"What's wrong?" gasped Charley.

Lizzie sighed. "*What's wrong?* We're in the military headquarters of an alien nation that wants to turn our planet into a leisure centre, and you want to know what's wrong?"

Charley scowled. "I didn't mean that and you know it," she hissed. "I mean, *why* are we hiding?"

"Because I think we should get out of here," said Lizzie. In her mind, she was still staring at the furious figure at the front of the room. At the thin, hard features and the pale, pale skin. Louis Zu: the Scourge of the Universe; the Emperor of Wei.

"But Mrs Moscos said we should do what she told us," argued Charley. "If she left us here, then here is where she wants us to be."

Lizzie didn't answer for a few seconds. She was imagining Louis Zu with a black umbrella tucked under one arm and a grey hat on his head. She could see him opening the door to Kosmickicks. She could see him vanishing inside. Now she knew why she hadn't been able to find him in the shop. Now she knew why he'd never come out again. He'd been on his way to Wei!

"That's not Louis Zu," Lizzie finally said very softly. She turned to her friend, "That's Mr Whisper!"

"Oh, please," Charley groaned. "I know a lot of weird things have happened today, but that's too weird. Besides, you can't even see his face properly from back here."

"I know it's Mr Whisper," insisted Lizzie. "I just *know* it is."

Charley groaned again. "You're hallucinating from shock, Lizzie. Mr Whisper's an accountant, not a ruler of galaxies." She started edging her way back to where they'd been standing. "I think we should obey Mrs Moscos, even if it seems like a bad idea."

"I'm telling you, it's Mr Whisper," Lizzie protested. She was so surprised that she wasn't afraid any more. Mr Whisper, the meekest and mildest man on Meteor Drive, was planning to conquer the Earth.

Charley, hesitating at the side of the walkway, looked towards the roaring figure of Louis Zu.

"Good grief!" she gasped. She turned to Lizzie. "It *is* Mr Whisper! Lizzie, what if he recognizes us?"

"That's what I've been trying to tell you!" snapped Lizzie. "We have to get out of here!"

Trying to get Charley back behind the console, Lizzie pulled her arm. But she pulled too hard, and they crashed into the wall behind them.

"I don't believe this is happening," said Charley as the wall opened and they tumbled through.

Out of the Burgermobile and into the Zoo

Lizzie and Charley landed in a heap on the other side of the door, which closed behind them even before they got to their feet.

"Now what do we do?" asked Charley.

Lizzie looked around. They were in another long corridor with silver walls.

"We try to get out of here, that's what we do," said Lizzie. "Mr Whisper is waiting to meet Harry the Rabbit's friends, and it'd be better if he didn't find out that we're them."

Trying to be brave for Charley, who was trying to be brave for her, Lizzie lead the way forward until they came to another hallway that intersected the one they were in.

Charley squeezed her hand. "I hear footsteps," she whispered.

Lizzie held her breath. She heard footsteps, too. Clickclickclickclickclickclick... They seemed to be coming from the left. She peered round the edge of the wall.

"What is it?" whispered Charley.

"Jit guards," said Lizzie. "Dozens of them!"

Charley clenched her hands nervously. "Now what are we going to do?"

It didn't seem to Lizzie that they really had much choice. There was nowhere to hide. If they turned themselves in to the Jits, the Jits would realize that they hadn't had the transportation gas. Then it wouldn't matter if Mr Whisper recognized them or not. They would never see home again. All they could do was pretend that they had had the transportation gas and hope for the best.

"Nothing," said Lizzie. "We're just going to stand here as though we're in a trance."

Crossing her fingers, Lizzie stiffened her body and stared straight ahead as the clicking heels of the Jit guards came closer.

Eyes straight ahead, looking neither right nor left, six Jits marched past. Behind them were three children from the birthday party, still clutching balloons. They were joined to the guards by a thin, blue band of light. From the way the children were beginning to look around and smile, Lizzie guessed that the first phase of the transportation gas must be wearing off.

"I wonder where they're taking them," whispered Charley.

"I know where they're *not* taking them," answered Lizzie. "They're going in the opposite direction to Mr Whisper."

It was as she said "They're going in the opposite direction to Mr Whisper," that Lizzie had her idea. If they joined the other children, the guards might not notice that there were two more. They might take them to somewhere where they'd be safe for a while. At least long enough to think of a plan.

"Come on," said Lizzie, grabbing hold of Charley. "Let's get behind them."

Charley, however, thought less of this idea than Lizzie did. "Do what? Why don't we just turn ourselves in?"

"Because then they'd know we haven't had the gas," Lizzie said. "Come on, there's nothing to lose."

Clickclickclickclickclickclick...

Thumpthumpthump...

Lizzie wasn't sure which was loudest: the beating of her heart or the steps of the Jit guards who were silently leading her, Charley, and the children from the birthday party through a maze of corridors, none of which seemed to have either a beginning or an end. The only break in the monotony of those endless hallways was the occasional handleless door that opened without being touched.

Lizzie concentrated on trying to remember the route they were taking. She knew from films that heroes always made sure they knew the way out. Left ... right ... right ... door ... right ... left... left ... door... But she wasn't very good at mazes. When she and Charley went to Hampton Court maze, Charley had to send the ticket collector in to lead Lizzie out. The headquarters of the Wei government were similar to Hampton Court in that respect. Every corridor looked just like the last. She had a hard time keeping track.

Clickclickclickclickclickclick...

Thumpthumpthump...

At first the corridors were crowded with Weis. Some of them sailed past as though they hadn't noticed the five human children surrounded by Jits; others stopped to look at them. Lizzie couldn't understand what they said, but she knew from the way they nudged each other and laughed that they were talking about them.

The further the guards took them, however, the emptier the hallways became; until at last Lizzie, Charley, the children and their escorts were all alone again.

Right ... right ... left ... left...

Clickclickclickclickclickclick...

Thumpthumpthump...

Lizzie was trying to remember if they'd gone left or right at the last turning when she realized that they'd left the silver corridors and were walking through a tunnel of glass. Something flickered in the wall on her right.

The guards were looking straight ahead. Lizzie glanced over. It was all she could do not to gasp out loud. Behind the glass walls were living creatures, gazing back through the windows of their cells with uncurious eyes. Lizzie realized what this meant. They must be in Louis Zu's private, intergalactic zoo!

The guards' pace didn't slow as they marched past the exhibits. Out of the corner of her eye, Lizzie read the sign in each cell as she passed it. Gvarks. Gvarks looked rather like very large reptiles in gold lamé suits. Simkas were slender and green with eyes like blue marbles. The Loons were small with enormous ears. The furry ones were Bimks. Lizzie had just absorbed the fact that the fat, white animal with the black face was a sheep when the guards made a turn that took them to a small black door. The door opened, and the five children were sucked inside the way dust is sucked into a hoover.

The room Lizzie and Charley found themselves in was large, brightly lit, and filled with chairs and tables. Besides the chairs and tables, the room was filled with people. Some of them were standing in queues that led to a group of Happy Burger employees, who were bustling back and forth in front of them; others were shuffling around as though looking for tables or carrying trays; others were sitting down. The room echoed with their laughter and talk.

"What are they doing?" whispered Lizzie.

"Well…" Charley hesitated. "Some of them seem to be eating."

It was true that some of the people did seem to be eating. Just as the people in the pink and green uniforms were going through the motions of making and serving hamburgers, some of the others were taking things off imaginary trays; they were opening imaginary packets; they were lifting their empty hands to their mouths; they were chewing invisible food.

"What do you think this is?" asked Lizzie. "Some kind of play?" Her parents often watched plays on TV that were just as strange as this.

"No," said Charley, her voice so soft Lizzie could barely hear her. "I don't think it's a play."

Lizzie looked over to where the three children who had come in with them were now sitting at a corner table, pretending to throw food at one another. She turned round. There, right in front of her, was a glass wall. She was just in time to see the silver uniform and purple motorcycle helmet of a Jit disappear out of view.

"Oh, my God..." Suddenly Lizzie realized where they were. She gulped as though swallowing a very large pill. "Charley! We're on the wrong side of Louis Zu's zoo!"

Charley's voice sounded very far away. "Then these must be the people from the Happy Burger. They must be in the second phase of the transportation gas."

Lizzie absorbed this new information. If these were the people from the Happy Burger, then Allie and Gemma must be—

"Over there!" Charley grabbed her arm. She'd obviously come to the same conclusion. "Lizzie, look over there!"

Allie and Gemma were standing at the back of one of the long queues. Allie was gesturing with her hands, and Gemma was smiling. Both of them were talking.

The zoo and the guards and Louis Zu vanished from Lizzie's mind. All she could think of was Allie and Gemma. There they were, just across the cell, reliving ten minutes of their lives that had happened hours ago and millions of light-years away! Lizzie nearly shouted with joy. Allie couldn't see or hear her! This was the opportunity she'd been waiting for since she first realized what a pain in the bum her sister was.

"Where are you going?" asked Charley.

Lizzie was already half-way to the queue.

"I just have to see something…"

She stopped beside her sister and listened. Allie and Gemma were talking about some boy. Normally, Lizzie would have done anything to overhear Allie and Gemma in one of their private conversations, but right now she couldn't care less.

Hesitantly at first, Lizzie waved a hand in front of her sister's eyes. Allie kept right on talking. Lizzie became a little less hesitant. She blew in her sister's ear. Allie laughed and leaned her head against Gemma's.

Lizzie could barely contain her excitement. This was as good as being invisible! She put her hands next to her sister's head and flapped them up and down.

"Lizzie!" Charley tugged on her sleeve.

But Lizzie was having too much fun to pay any attention to Charley. "Isn't this excellent? I wish I had a video camera. Nobody's going to believe this."

"Lizzie!" Charley's hiss was shrill. "Lizzie, *please* … look at the window!"

Reluctantly, Lizzie looked. Two Jits had stationed themselves in front of the cell. They were gazing in fascination through the glass. They looked as though they would have liked a video camera, too.

"Now what do we do?" wailed Charley.

There was only one thing they could do: enter phase two of the transportation gas. Putting a thoughtful expression on her face, Lizzie pointed to the wall and pretended to read the menu.

Lizzie Takes Charge

···

The queue of zombie hamburger eaters shuffled forward as it did every few minutes. Lizzie and Charley shuffled forward with it.

"We're never going to get out of here, are we?" moaned Charley. "We're going to be stuck here trying to decide what to order for the rest of our lives."

Lizzie sighed. She'd been thinking that very same thing herself. But she wasn't about to admit it to Charley. She didn't need to have Charley blaming her again.

"Of course we'll get out of here," said Lizzie. She thought she sounded pretty convincing. "Mrs Moscos wouldn't abandon us on an alien planet."

"*She* didn't abandon *us*," said Charley bitterly. "If I remember correctly, *we* abandoned *her*."

"We did no such thing," said Lizzie. "We couldn't let Mr Whisper get close enough to recognize us, and you know it. Anyway," she went on stubbornly, "Mrs Moscos will be back. She's a very responsible person."

"Is she? She grows onions in her front garden," said Charley, as though this settled the matter.

"She always waters our plants when we go on holiday," countered Lizzie. "And she looks after the Mahoneys' dog when they go away." Surely a person who could be counted on by her neighbours wasn't the sort of person to leave two little girls all alone in deepest space. Was she?

But Charley wasn't impressed by Mrs Moscos's performance as a good neighbour. "Then where is she?" she demanded. "I'm getting really tired of this."

Lizzie stared at the imaginary menu on the wall and sighed. Where *was* Mrs Moscos? Why hadn't she returned? The sigh turned to a moan as another depressing thought occurred to her: that Mrs Moscos hadn't come back because she couldn't.

"Maybe Mrs Moscos's been captured by Louis Zu," suggested Lizzie.

Charley turned to her with her mouth opened and her eyes wide. "You don't really think that, do you?"

Lizzie nodded. How many films had she seen where the hero was patiently waiting to be rescued by someone who was being held at gunpoint somewhere else? The more Lizzie thought about it, the more it seemed to her that there couldn't be any other explanation.

"I think we should get out of here," she said. "I think we should try and find Mrs Moscos." She couldn't help smiling. She'd really be a hero if she saved Mrs Moscos.

"Out?" Charley continued to gape. "Have you gone totally mad? How are we going to get out of here?"

Lizzie smiled. She'd already worked this out. "Through the heating ducts," she announced happily.

Charley frowned. "The heating ducts?" She sounded as though she wasn't quite sure what heating ducts were.

Lizzie wasn't quite sure what heating ducts were, either, but that didn't bother her. "Yeah, the heating ducts. You know…" coaxed Lizzie. "In films, the hero always escapes by crawling through the heating ducts. We'll be able to go wherever we want without anyone knowing we're there. That way we can find where they're holding Mrs Moscos and rescue her."

Charley scrunched her lips together. "I was hoping Mrs Moscos was going to rescue us."

Lizzie rolled her eyes. "She can't rescue us if she's being held prisoner, can she? It's up to us to save her."

"What about the guards?" Charley asked warily.

"The guards aren't even watching any more," said Lizzie. This was true. The Jits had turned their backs to the window. "They won't even know we're gone," she added with her old confidence.

Charley looked hopeful. "Are you sure?"

"Positive." Lizzie started edging towards the wall in search of an opening that would lead to the ducts. She couldn't wait to see the expression on Mrs Moscos's face when she and Charley turned up to save her.

But Charley still wasn't totally convinced. Her eyes darted round the room. "I don't see any vents, maybe the Weis don't watch the same films as you."

"'They've got to be here somewhere," Lizzie insisted. She wasn't just going to be a citizen of the cosmos, she was going to be a hero of the cosmos as well.

With one eye on the guards, she started to make her way around the room. She slipped past the crowded tables and ducked between the families looking for seats. She peered behind everyone who was blocking a wall. But Charley was right: there were no vents that might lead to freedom.

Charley was standing with her arms folded

and a smug look on her face when Lizzie got back. "Didn't I tell you?" she asked.

"It's not fair," complained Lizzie. "There's always a way out in the films."

Charley pointed to a small rectangle in the wall. "Well, what about that door then?" she asked.

"That's the door we came in," said Lizzie. No hero she'd ever heard of went out the way they'd come in.

Charley didn't seem to know this. "So?"

The little patience Lizzie had left vanished as quickly as Mrs Moscos had. "So, not only does it not have a handle, but it'll be locked," she snapped. "Do you think the Weis leave the cages of their zoo open in case the exhibits want to take a walk?"

Charley didn't answer. She was getting ready to throw herself at the door.

"Well, do you?" demanded Lizzie.

Charley screamed.

Lizzie looked round in time to see her best friend topple from the room.

As it turned out, the door Charley fell through was not the door they'd come in by. Instead of finding themselves back in the maze of corridors, they found themselves in a metal tunnel that ran under the floors.

"I don't like this," whispered Charley nervously. "I can't see a thing."

"I really think I should be in front," hissed Lizzie as she crawled through the dark behind Charley. "My eyesight's better than yours." Which was technically true. Charley wore glasses for reading. Besides, how was Lizzie going to be a hero if Charley got to Mrs Moscos first?

"So get in front of me, then," snapped Charley. "I didn't ask to lead, did I?"

"And I didn't tell you to fall through the door," Lizzie snapped back.

Charley had been moving incredibly slowly before, now she came to a dead stop. "So go on," she ordered. "Get ahead of me."

Unfortunately, getting ahead of Charley was more easily said than done. The tunnel was not only dark, it was narrow as well. Every time Lizzie moved she hit Charley.

"Ow!" cried Charley. "Watch what you're doing! You nearly poked out my eye."

"Well, make yourself thinner or something," grunted Lizzie.

Charley jabbed her with her knee. "You make yourself thinner. You're the one who wants to lead."

Lizzie sucked in her stomach and held her breath, straining every muscle as she tried to drag herself past Charley.

"It's no use," she gasped. "Maybe if you lie flat, and I crawl over you..."

"Anything," said Charley, flattening herself out face down. "I just want to get out of here."

Inch by inch, Lizzie pulled herself over the grunting Charley until at last her chin was resting on Charley's head.

"Well, go on," urged Charley in a very muffled voice. "I can't breathe with you on top of me like this."

"I can't move," said Lizzie. "I'm stuck."

"You *can't* be stuck." Although Charley's voice was muffled, it was sharp with panic.

"Yes, I can," said Lizzie miserably. Her shoulders were wedged between Charley and the tunnel.

"Well, do something," ordered Charley. "If you can't go forward then back off."

Lizzie started to do something. She pressed her head and shoulders against the top of the tunnel.

In films the hero always came down through the ceiling. But Lizzie wasn't in a film. She was in the headquarters of the government of Wei.

Lizzie came up through the floor.

Wei Is a Place of Surprises

....

Lizzie reached her hand through the trap
door to help Charley out.

"I told you it would work," she said hauling
Charley on to the floor beside her. She
couldn't help feeling pretty pleased with
herself. It just showed how wrong her mother
was when she said Lizzie watched too much
television.

Charley rubbed her knees and blinked.
"Where are we?" she whispered.

Lizzie looked round. She'd been so
surprised and so relieved to be out of the
tunnel that, apart from making sure that
there were no Weis around, she hadn't really
thought about where they were.

There were actually two answers to
Charley's question. The first was that they
were in a room the size of a cupboard. The

second was that Lizzie had no idea where they were.

"Who cares?" she said. "We're out, aren't we? Now all we have to do is find Mrs Moscos and we'll be on our way home."

Charley looked at Lizzie as though she had suddenly grown an extra head. "Just like that?" asked Charley. "We'll just walk out of here, find Mrs Moscos and take the next bus home?"

But Lizzie wasn't going to let Charley dampen her good mood. They'd escaped from the zoo and made it through the tunnel. She was going to be a hero, after all.

"No," she said, "we won't take a bus, we'll take the next Happy Burger home." She tiptoed the few steps to the door and put her ear against it.

Charley came up behind her. "Can you hear anything?"

Lizzie shook her head. "Not a thing." She stepped back. "You try."

Charley pressed her ear against the metal

surface. "I can't hear anything either," she whispered.

Lizzie took a deep breath. "Well," she said in true hero-fashion, "I guess there's only one thing to do then." Cautiously she pushed the door. Nothing happened.

"You have to throw yourself against it," directed Charley.

"I just want to open it a crack, not catapult through." Lizzie frowned in thought. The Weis didn't even touch doors to open them; they just held up their hands. Maybe it was heat that controlled them. Lizzie placed her palms flat on the silver surface. Very slowly, it started to move. She peered through the crack and found herself staring into a small room, with doors at each end.

"What is it?" whispered Charley.

Lizzie opened the door a little wider. "Nothing." Except for a few chairs and low tables and a series of photographs of unfamiliar planets on the walls, the room was empty. "It looks like a waiting room."

Charley's head appeared over Lizzie's shoulder. "There aren't any magazines," said Charley. "All the waiting rooms I've ever been in have old magazines lying around."

"All the waiting rooms you've ever been in have been on Earth," answered Lizzie as she stepped into the room.

Charley hurried after her.

"You check the door on the right," ordered Lizzie. "I'll check the one on the left."

She tiptoed across the room and put her ear to the door. Once again, there was only silence. "I can't hear anything," she called to Charley. "What about you?"

Charley shook her head. "Nothing," she reported. "What do you think we should do?"

Lizzie looked from one door to the other. "We'll have to pick one, and open it. You know, like that guy in the fairytale."

Charley looked from the one door to the other. "Which one?" she asked nervously. Charley knew the fairytale. Behind one door was a mountain of gold; behind the other was a three-headed monster that hadn't eaten for several decades.

Lizzie eyed the doors again. Which door held the solution to all their problems, and which the hungry monster?

"We'll flip," she decided, taking a coin from her pocket and holding it in the air. "Heads we open this door; tails we open yours."

Lizzie closed her eyes and tossed.

"Well?" hissed Charley.

"Heads."

Lizzie put the coin back in to her pocket. There was nothing to do now, but open the door. They were in the hands of Fate.

Charley stood beside her and together they raised their hands.

"One…"

"Two…"

"Three…"

They placed their palms on the metal surface. The door opened so quickly that they fell straight into the next room without any warning.

Lizzie and Charley held on to each other as the door closed behind them.

"Uh oh…" whispered Lizzie, holding on to Charley. Fate, it seemed, had made the wrong choice.

Sitting in one of the chairs, with his feet up on a silver table and a bunch of balloons floating over his head, was Harry the Rabbit.

Lizzie gave Charley a nudge. "I suppose I'm hallucinating that, too."

Charley nudged her back. "Don't start on me," she warned.

"Ladies, please…" said Harry the Rabbit. "We have no time for bickering."

Lizzie and Charley froze. The voice was muffled, but it was unmistakable.

"Mrs Moscos!" cried Lizzie."What are you doing here?"

"Oh, Mrs Moscos!" Charley was practically sobbing with relief. "I was afraid you'd abandoned us!"

Harry the Rabbit's balloons bobbed. "Of course I wouldn't abandon you," snapped

Mrs Moscos. "But I had to get the transporter, didn't I?"

"You didn't have to tell them we were friends of Harry the Rabbit," protested Lizzie. "You didn't have to leave us with Louis Zu."

"Nonsense," said Mrs Moscos smartly. "Of course I did. The fastest way to find out where the humans were kept was to let them take you there."

The Fate of the World Is in Lizzie Wesson's Hands

Pleased as Lizzie and Charley were to have found Mrs Moscos, they were even happier to be able to tell her their news.

"Mrs Moscos! Mrs Moscos!" they cried excitedly. "Mrs Moscos, guess what?"

"We have no time for guessing games," said Mrs Moscos crisply.

Charley and Lizzie tugged on her paws.

"But this is really fantastic," said Charley.

"That's right," agreed Lizzie. "You won't believe it."

With a heavy sigh, Mrs Moscos folded her giant furry arms in front of her. "All right, I give up. What have you discovered?"

"It's Mr Whisper," they told her proudly. "Mr Whisper is Louis Zu!"

When Mrs Moscos didn't immediately share in their excitement, or even give any sign of having heard them, Lizzie went on. "No, it's true, Mrs Moscos. It really is."

The giant ears bobbed in their direction. "That's it? Louis Zu is minutes away from walking through that door, and you waste my time telling me things I already know?" She glared at them through the eye holes in Harry the Rabbit's neck. "You saw Mr Whisper going into Kosmickicks, didn't you? What did you think he was doing, buying a disco shirt?"

Lizzie and Charley exchanged looks.

"What *was* he doing?" they asked.

"He was moving his Weis into Happy Burger through the tunnel in the basement, of course," said Mrs Moscos, as though they should have known this too. She clapped her paws together. "Now, if you don't mind, Louis Zu will be with us very shortly. He has been looking for you two ever since you disappeared from the control room. It would be better if I were alone when he arrives."

"Where are we supposed to go?" asked Charley.

"Maybe she expects us to become invisible," mumbled Lizzie.

Harry's glassy eyes turned on her. "We have no time for your grumbling, Lizzie Wesson. You and Charley must go back to the zoo. If I don't join you within ten minutes, you must return to Earth with the other humans." She removed something from the pocket of Harry's baggy green trousers and handed it to Lizzie.

"What is it?" asked Lizzie. "Some kind of remote control?"

"That," said Mrs Moscos, "is the most sophisticated intergalactic transporter in the cosmos."

Charley frowned. "Where did you get it?"

"It was on Louis Zu's desk in the control room," Mrs Moscos smiled. "Carelessness is another of the human habits he's acquired over the centuries." She stopped smiling. "But there is no time for chatting now. At exactly thirty-four hundred hours, Wei time, I want you to push the purple button. That will take you back to the shopping centre."

Lizzie stared at the box in her hand. It had a torch at one end, a digital clock set on Wei time, and more coloured buttons than her remote control at home. "But what do I do when we get there?" she asked.

"You don't have to do anything. It's set up as a chain reaction," said Mrs Moscos as though the answer was so obvious she couldn't imagine why Lizzie had asked the question. "But you must push the purple button at exactly thirty-four hundred hours. There isn't much margin on these things, I'm afraid. A few nanoseconds in either direction and you could transport yourself to a different time."

"But Mrs Moscos," cut in Charley, "how are we going to get back to the zoo?"

In answer, Mrs Moscos put a furry paw on each of their shoulders and gave them a shove towards the door. "You will go back the way you came, through the emergency escape tunnel," she said crisply.

Charley looked at Lizzie. *So that's what it was!*

"It was very clever of you to realize that you could get to anywhere in the building through it," Mrs Moscos went on more warmly. She pushed them through the door that had silently opened in front of them.

Lizzie knew she should ask how they'd know when they reached the humans' cage, but she wasn't sure that it was the sort of question a hero would ask. Fortunately, Charley wasn't trying to be a hero. She just wanted to get home.

"But Mrs Moscos," said Charley, "how will we know when we're at the right place?"

"Listen!" said Mrs Moscos as the door closed in front of her. "Listen…"

The strong, steady beam of the transporter light cut through the darkness ahead to reveal even more darkness.

"I'm listening," Charley whispered between grunts as they crawled along, "but I can't hear anything except my heart pounding and my bones being bruised."

Clutching the intergalactic transporter in

one hand, Lizzie slowly dragged herself forward. Being a hero wasn't as much fun as it looked in films. "It might help if we actually knew what we're meant to be listening for," she grumbled. Although Lizzie understood that she and Charley had to get away before Louis Zu saw them, she thought Mrs Moscos could have been a little more informative. Lizzie hadn't even had a chance to ask her about Mr Whisper.

"Wait a minute!" cried Charley. "I think I do hear something."

Lizzie stopped and listened. Charley was right. She could just make out the sound of giggling above them.

"This must be it!" said Lizzie with a certain amount of relief. "That's got to be Allie and Gemma." She played the transporter torch on the ceiling. Sure enough, directly over their heads was the outline of a trap door.

Lizzie passed the transporter to Charley and put both hands on the door. "Push," she ordered.

Charley pushed.

Lizzie rose through the floor, blinking in the sudden light. Once again she had the unpleasant sensation of falling through space. It wasn't Allie and Gemma giggling like that. It was hundreds of very small, downy creatures that looked remarkably like shuttlecocks. Their tiny bodies shaking with laughter, they rolled towards Lizzie like a tide of fluff.

"Wrong!" gasped Lizzie, dropping back through the door with amazing speed

"What is it?" asked Charley.

Lizzie shook her head. "I don't know," she said, still in some shock. "But I'm pretty sure they don't eat–" Her words trailed off as she finally realized what they were meant to be listening for.

"Don't eat what?" asked Charley.

"Hamburgers." Lizzie took back the transporter. "Don't eat hamburgers."

Charley scowled. "What's that supposed to mean?"

Lizzie grinned, just like a hero who's finally broken the enemy code. "It means that we listen for the sound of people ordering fast food."

Not that long ago, Lizzie would have said that she never wanted to be in one of Louis Zu's cages again, but now that she and Charley were back among the humans she was feeling pretty happy. They were safe, they were about to go home and, most importantly, they were about to become heroes.

"Can you believe it, Charley?" Lizzie couldn't help smiling. "We did it! We saved the world!"

Charley didn't smile back. "We're not out of this galaxy yet," she said, her eyes going from the guards at the window to the door they were expecting Mrs Moscos to march through at any second. "You still have to push the button, remember."

Lizzie nodded. She hadn't forgotten about the button. She was a hero, wasn't she?

Heroes remembered things like that.

"Thirty-four hundred hours, Wei time," said Lizzie. She held the clock on the transporter so Charley could see. "Just ten more seconds, or whatever they are, to go."

Charley nodded, and glanced at the door again. "I wonder if Mrs Moscos's going to make it," she worried.

"Six…" said Lizzie.

Charley glanced at the window. "Oh, my gosh," she said, "there's Mrs Moscos."

"Right on time," said Lizzie, her finger over the purple button and her eye on the clock. "She'd better hurry."

"But she's with Louis Zu!" said Charley. "They're in the Burgermobile."

Lizzie looked up. The Burgermobile was parked by the guards. Louis Zu was giving orders, but Harry the Rabbit was gazing into the humans' cage, his paw waving up and down ever so slightly.

"She's telling you to push the button," said Charley. "Lizzie, look! Mrs Moscos's telling you to push the button."

Lizzie glanced back at the clock: thirty-four hundred hours exactly. "But we can't go without her," argued Lizzie. A good hero never left anybody behind.

"But she wants you to!" shrieked Charley. "Lizzie, push the button!"

The fluorescent numbers on the clock moved to thirty-four hundred hours and one … and three … and six. Lizzie's finger continued to hover over the purple button.

"I can't do it." She looked back at Harry the Rabbit. Louis Zu was helping Harry out of the Burgermobile. The balloons had got tangled in the awning, and Louis Zu was trying to free them. He was smiling. Lizzie wondered why that didn't make her feel any better.

"Push the button, will you?" screamed Charley. "We're going to wind up back in the Roman Empire if you don't hurry."

Harry the Rabbit was only inches from the window. Unfortunately, he was paw in hand with Louis Zu. Lizzie's finger remained in the air. Unable to stand it any more, Charley grabbed the transporter and pushed the button herself.

Half expecting to see a group of Roman soldiers coming towards her, Lizzie looked around unhappily. She'd had her chance to be a hero, and what had she done? As usual, she hadn't done what she was told, that's what she'd done. Thanks to her, the Earth was going to become a theme park and all the people on it would become attractions. Lizzie didn't like to think what her parents were going to say about that.

She was so upset that it took her a few seconds to realize she was staring at the green door of the Happy Burger toilet. The transporter had worked! Beside herself with joy, Lizzie hurried out of the cubicle.

"Charley?" called Lizzie. "Charley, are you all right?"

The door to Charley's stall opened slowly. "I think so," said Charley shakily. "How about you?"

"I'm fine." Lizzie looked round the pink and green room. Everything was exactly as it had been when they first entered. She raised her head. There were no speakers in the ladies, but she could still hear the music that was playing upstairs.

"It's weird, isn't it?" asked Charley. "It feels like we've never been away."

Lizzie had the same feeling. She wasn't even sure now why she'd thought there might be Romans in the Happy Burger ladies.

Charley looked at her watch. "Good grief... It's ten to six! That means we've moved ahead in time because you wouldn't push the button." A look of fresh panic came over her face. "And that means that your sister's been waiting for us for nearly an hour!"

"Unless she left without us," said Lizzie, hopefully. At least if Allie had gone home, Lizzie and Charley would have a chance to talk about what had happened before everyone started screaming at them.

"What do you mean, 'Unless she left without us'?" said Charley. "How could she leave without us? She was with us on Wei!"

Allie hadn't left without them. She and Gemma were waiting in front of Kosmic-kicks, tapping their feet and scowling. Allie started shouting the instant she saw Lizzie.

"Where have you two been?" she yelled. "Do you know what time it is? Gemma and I have been waiting over an hour for you!"

Lizzie glanced at Charley. Allie and Gemma remembered nothing of what had happened. Unfortunately, the thought made Lizzie smile.

"Don't you smirk at me, you termite!" screamed Allie. Her face had been flushed before, but now it was almost purple with rage. "You just wait till we get home. You just wait till I tell Mum what you did."

"She'd better calm down," whispered Charley. "She's going to burst a blood vessel, or something."

But Lizzie wasn't worried about Allie. She

couldn't wait to get home and tell her parents what she'd done, either. She'd saved the world! She wouldn't be surprised if they took her out to dinner to celebrate.

"We can explain everything," said Lizzie calmly.

Allie, however, was beyond explanations. "Don't even speak to me," she ordered "I just want to get home."

As they followed Allie and Gemma to the bus stop, Charley whispered, "The only thing worse than having to face your sister is having to face my mother. She's going to throw a fit when she finds out what happened."

Lizzie gave her an astonished look. "What's wrong with you?" she demanded. "Your mother isn't going to be cross, she's going to be happy." Lizzie grinned. "Don't you get it? You and I are heroes, Charley. We saved the Earth from a fate worse than death."

Charley shook her head. "I don't know…" she said slowly. "I mean, let's face it, Lizzie, who's going to believe us?" She looked around them at the car park and the bus queues and the mob of people with packages in their arms. "I'm finding it a little hard to believe myself."

Lizzie didn't want to admit that she was finding it a little hard, too, but the further they got from Happy Burger, the more she began to wonder if everything she remembered happening really had. Nothing on the Earth had changed. Not the Happy Burger, not Allie and Gemma, not the shopping centre, not even Charley.

"But Mrs Moscos—" began Lizzie.

"We don't even know where Mrs Moscos is," interrupted Charley as she got on to the bus. "Though I suppose we'll know we weren't dreaming if she never comes back to Meteor Drive."

"Let me get this straight," said Lizzie's mother. She looked at Lizzie's father, then back at Lizzie. "You and Charley kept your sister waiting for two hours because you had to go to another planet to save the Earth."

Allie giggled.

"Allie, please," said Lizzie's father.

"It wasn't two hours," argued Lizzie. "We were meant to meet them at four-thirty, and they didn't turn up till after five."

"You mean you didn't turn up till nearly six!" shrieked Allie.

'Allie, please!" Lizzie's father took a deep breath. "So where were you while your sister was waiting for you?" he asked more gently.

"I told you," said Lizzie. "We were on Wei. We—"

"Lizzie…" Her mother looked very tired. "You can't possibly expect us to believe that you spent the afternoon on an alien planet. Why don't you just admit that you and Charley completely forgot about the time, and then…"

"You'll be grounded for the rest of your life," broke in Allie.

Lizzie made a lunge for her sister just as the doorbell rang.

Mr Wesson sighed. "Now who on earth could that be?"

Lizzie was still trying to get at her sister when she heard Mrs Moscos's voice at the door. She dropped her hands and turned in surprise.

"I'm so sorry to disturb you," Mrs Moscos was saying to Mr Wesson, "but I bumped into Lizzie and Charley in the shopping centre when I went to pick up my new remote control. I took Lizzie's carrier bag by mistake and I'm afraid she must have gone off with the remote control..."

Everyone turned to Lizzie.

"...in her pocket," said Mrs Moscos, stepping into the room. Lizzie's eyes shifted from Mrs Moscos to her mother as she removed the transporter from her pocket and handed it over to Mrs Moscos. She was feeling a little stunned.

"I'm afraid that 'bump' is the most exact word," Mrs Moscos continued with a laugh. "I wasn't looking where I was going and I walked right into Lizzie." She smiled brightly. "Didn't I, Lizzie?"

Lizzie managed a nod.

Mrs Moscos turned to Lizzie's mother. "Actually, I don't know what I would have done without Lizzie and Charley," said Mrs Moscos. "They wouldn't leave me till I'd seen the nurse and had my ankle bandaged."

Lizzie stared at the ankle Mrs Moscos was holding up for everyone to see. There was a neat beige bandage wrapped around it.

"Are you sure you should be walking on it?" asked Mrs Wesson.

"That's just what Lizzie said," said Mrs Moscos. "But I wouldn't hear of her taking me any further than the bus stop. It's only a sprain, after all."

Lizzie's mother looked over at Lizzie. "Why didn't you say you were with Mrs Moscos?" she asked.

"But I *did* say I was with Mrs Moscos!" protested Lizzie.

Mrs Wesson laughed. "Kids," she said to

Mrs Moscos. "Lizzie's been trying to convince us that you took her and Charley to an alien planet this afternoon. She almost had me believing that she believed it."

Mrs Moscos laughed delightedly. "What a wonderful imagination she has," said Mrs Moscos. She started back towards the door.

Lizzie followed her.

"Oh, I almost forgot," said Mrs Moscos. She thrust a black carrier into Lizzie's hands.

"But Mrs Moscos," hissed Lizzie. "Mrs Moscos, what happened?"

"Nothing," Mrs Moscos smiled. "Which is just what we wanted, isn't it?"

Lizzie watched Mrs Moscos walk down the Wessons' front path and into her own garden. When she'd disappeared inside, Lizzie looked down at the bag she was holding. It said KOSMICKICKS in silver letters. And under that, London – Paris – New York – Yurn. Inside was a black top. Across its front in silver were the words *Next Time I Really Will Do as I'm Told*.

HARRY THE EXPLORER
by Dyan Sheldon

It's a wet afternoon and Chicken is doing a jigsaw puzzle. Harry, her cat, is bored – so he twitches his ears to make something interesting happen. For Harry is no ordinary cat, he's an extraterrestrial being in disguise! Suddenly the back garden has turned into the lake of the jigsaw puzzle and, in no time at all, Chicken finds herself rowing Harry across it! The result, as usual, is trouble with a capital T!

CREEPE HALL
by Alan Durant

"A rollicking read to sink your fangs into."
Young Telegraph

Sent to stay with distant relatives, Oliver finds himself at Creepe Hall, home to the weirdest, wackiest bunch of characters you could ever hope to meet!

"Vampires, ghosts and werebadgers... A fast-moving story – loads of fun, written with style and humour." *Books for Keeps*

"An amusing, gently prodding tale in the Addams family tradition."
The Independent on Sunday

MORE WALKER PAPERBACKS

For You to Enjoy